For Claire Weir
M.W.

For Dinah
A.B.

First published 1990 by
Walker Books Ltd, 87 Vauxhall Walk, London SE11 5HJ

Text © 1990 Martin Waddell   Illustrations © 1990 Angela Barrett

4 6 8 10 9 7 5 3

This book has been typeset in Berkeley Medium Oldstyle.

Printed in Hong Kong

British Library Cataloguing in Publication Data
A catalogue record for this book is
available from the British Library.

ISBN 0-7445-1266-2

The Hidden House

Written by Martin Waddell ∽ Illustrated by Angela Barrett

WALKER BOOKS

AND SUBSIDIARIES

LONDON • BOSTON • SYDNEY

In a little house, down a little lane, lived an old man.

His name was Bruno.

He was very lonely in the little house, so he made wooden dolls to keep him company.

He made three of them. The knitting one is Maisie, the one with the spade is Ralph, and the one with the pack on his back is Winnaker.

They sat on Bruno's window ledge and watched him working in his garden, growing potatoes and cabbages and parsnips and beans.

Bruno talked to them sometimes, but not very much. They were wooden dolls and they couldn't talk back, and Bruno wasn't stupid. The dolls didn't talk, but I *think* they were happy.

One day Bruno went away and didn't come back.

Everything changed, slowly.

Wild things covered the lane and climbed all over Bruno's fence. Brambles choked the garden, and ivy crept in through the window of the little house and spread about inside. A pale tree grew in the kitchen.

Maisie and Ralph and Winnaker watched it happen from their window ledge and they got dusty. They watched and watched, until the spiders spun up their window so that there was nothing left to see but webs. They didn't say anything, because they were wooden dolls, but I *think* they were lonely.

A mouse came by and nibbled Ralph's spade.

A beetle lived in Maisie's basket
for a day and then it went away.
An ant explored Winnaker but
didn't find anything.

Slowly, very slowly (it took years and years and years)
Bruno's little house disappeared in the middle of
green things.

It was still there, but nobody could see it. The house
was hidden, and Maisie and Ralph and Winnaker
were hidden inside it. I think they were watching.
There was a lot to see in the hidden house.

The house filled up with ants and beetles, mice and toads and creepy-crawlies, until it was fuller than it had ever been. Bees buzzed up the chimney, where the smoke used to be.

The little house grew warm and smelly with decay, but it was full of things happening.

Maisie and Ralph and Winnaker got damp and mildewed and turned a bit green, but I don't think they minded too much.

Then a man came down the lane and found the little house by poking his way in through the branches. He didn't spot Maisie and Ralph and Winnaker, because they were hidden in the ivy.

He liked the little house.

Next day he came again with his wife and daughter, and they explored the house and the garden, and liked it very much.

They said they'd come back, but a long time went by and they didn't come.

The hidden house had been forgotten again, and I *think* the wooden dolls were sad.

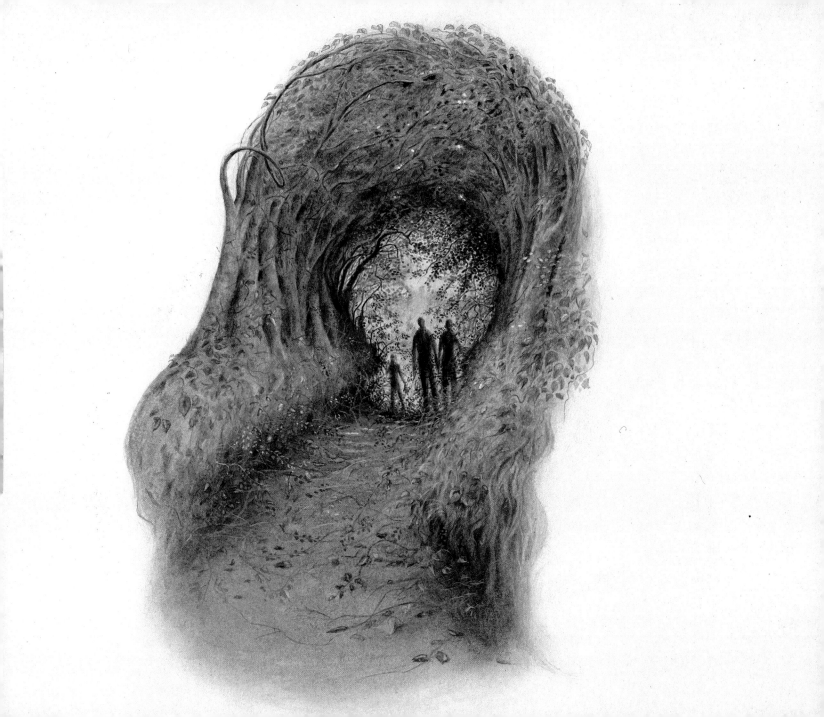

A whole winter
passed and
the house was
covered in snow.
Lots of things came
in from the wood
and hid there,
away from the cold.

Then, in the spring, the man came back with his wife and his little girl, and he brought a big axe. He cleared away the wildness round the little house. The man

and his wife and the little girl cleaned and cleared and hammered and nailed and painted and washed and brushed and *did* until everything was lovely.

The little girl found Maisie and Ralph and Winnaker. She got her paintbrush and painted them. Then she set them on the window ledge, looking out at the garden. The garden was filled with flowers. "There you are!" said the little girl. "A whole new world to look at." "A whole new family for them to look after," said the woman. "Our family," said the man, and he hugged his wife and daughter.

Maisie and Ralph and Winnaker didn't say a thing. They couldn't. They were wooden dolls. But now they had a whole family to live with, and I *think* they were happy again.